To my Mom and Dad: Thank you!

How to Use this Book

Helping Kids Realize the Power of their Brains to Be Happy and Successful!

The Best Gift
Big Scoop of Something

A Fun and Friendly Guide Teaching Kids
What It Means TO LOVE and TO BE LOVED!

An effective parenting tool, the FIND SOMETHING AWESOME! book series introduces kids to the powers (and fun!) of Positive Thinking, Gratitude, Mindfulness, and Focused Imagination. They will learn their own Awesome Brain Power to Be Happy and Successful!

Organized into five levels, each book stands alone and also builds on the concepts introduced in earlier levels.

Read the books together with your children, then discuss the concepts each level introduces using the Questions, Awesome Brain Capabilities, and Steps as a guide.

Happiness and Success start with FIND SOMETHING AWESOME!

www.mascotbooks.com

Big Scoop of Something

For more information, please contact:
Mascot Books
620 Herndon Parkway #320
Herndon, VA 20170
info@mascotbooks.com

Library of Congress Control Number: 2017915916

CPSIA Code: PRT0218A
ISBN: 978-1-68401-485-9

Printed in the United States

Find Something Awesome!

I AM AND I CAN!

MIND (BOX)

A BOOK SERIES

Helping Kids Realize the Power of their Brains to Be Happy and Successful!

The Best Gift

Big Scoop of Something

by **Matt Scott**

art by **Ana Sebastian**

www.FindSomethingAwesome.com

Please hold out your hand and make it palm up.
Curve all your fingers like making a cup.

I have something for you to take on your day,
Something quite useful as you go on your way!

This thing that I give is MAGICAL and TRUE,
You can use it for anything or everything you do!

I'll scoop it out of MY world and give it this day,
Like a big heap of ice cream to your cup, you could say!

Pretend to eat it, or smell it, or breathe it in deep,
This scoop that I give for sure is to keep!

Take this with you and WATCH what it'll do...

SOMETHING AWESOME WILL COME ON THIS DAY
JUST FOR YOU!

JANUARY

27	28	29	30	1	2	3
4	5	6	7	8	9	10
11	12	13	14	15	16	
18	19	20	21	22	23	
25	26	27	28	29	30	

Just set your brain knowing it does this this way,
And it will fuel Something Awesome to appear in your day!

You can look for ANYTHING awesome to find,

Or something SPECIFIC you seek
from your mind!

Each day as you leave, or even when still there,

I'll give you this scoop to do as you care!

This scoop that I give is truly MY LOVE,
A gift that I GIVE, I've learned from above.

So PLEASE use it and use it and use it all day!

And know that YOU CAN and IT WILL as I say!

No worry for wasting or using it all,
My source is as endless as the night sky is tall!

AWESOME CAPABILITIES

- You can USE our love to accomplish your dreams!
- You can accomplish anything you set your mind to!

AWESOME STEPS

- Believe!
- Know that we will always be loving you!

AWESOME QUESTIONS

- Who's awesome?
- Did you know that we think that you are AWESOME!
- What would be a really great goal to achieve?

ABOUT THE AUTHOR

"What I finally learned about true happiness as an adult, I wanted to teach kids early in life in a way that they could understand and use to get through the bumps of childhood and learn how to create their OWN happiness and success."

– Matt Scott

Matt Scott discovered the AWESOME power of our brains to find happiness and success. Now, he wants to share his discovery with all young people.

A Montana native, Matt is an active believer and dedicated reader of success and self-help books. He knows that EVERYONE'S brains are capable of creating a HAPPY and SUCCESSFUL life!

He says, **"Learning how our brains work in this world is IMPERATIVE to creating a happy and successful life!"** Matt was inspired to create the FIND SOMETHING AWESOME! book series to introduce and communicate the power of our brains in a universal way that could be understood and applied at an early age.

He wrote the series to give parents fun, yet powerful teaching tools to start the conversation, so all young people can have early knowledge of their brain's power to build self-confidence and learn how to create positive outcomes in life.

A happy childhood and successful adulthood starts with learning how to FIND SOMETHING AWESOME!

Matt loves his family, being a dad, and building friendships and community. He enjoys paddle boarding, snowboarding, and Air-Chairing! Matt lives in Los Angeles, California, with his wife and three children.

Find Something Awesome!

I AM AND I CAN!

MIND (BOX!)

A BOOK SERIES

Helping Kids Realize the Power of their Brains to Be Happy and Successful!

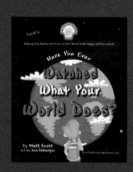

Recommended by Teachers, Therapists, Parents, & Kids!

What if you could give your children all the 'self-help' wisdom and life lessons you learned later in life in a book that they would actually love and listen to?

You can! FIND SOMETHING AWESOME! is a FUN and FRIENDLY book series that teaches kids the AWESOME power of their brains!

Kids will learn the necessary life skills to build self-confidence and create desired outcomes for Happiness and Success! This made-for-children series introduces the powers (and fun!) of Positive Thinking, Gratitude, Mindfulness, and Focused Imagination.

Building upon themselves, each book shows children what their brains are capable of doing!

Level 1: What Color Is Your Butterfly?
What we think affects how we feel! Kids will learn they can train their brain to 'FIND SOMETHING AWESOME!' to feel awesome!

Level 2: Have You Ever Thanked a Rainbow?
Gratitude leads to happiness! Helps kids understand the power (and fun!) of positive thinking and gratitude in everyday life.

Level 3: Did You Laugh When You Stubbed Your Toe?
Turn negative thinking around! Kids will learn how to recognize and turn off negative feelings, and to remain strong and confident with positive self-encouragement.

Level 4: Have You Ever Watched What Your World Does?
Positive Thinking, Gratitude, Self-encouragement, Mindfulness, and Focused Imagination lead to successful outcomes in life! Helps kids understand their brain's capabilities to help make their dreams come true!

Level 5: Where Do You Want To Go?
Imagine your dream! Kids will learn how to refuel themselves through loving their world to imagine and achieve their goals!

Do You Have a FIND SOMETHING AWESOME Story to Share?
We'd love to hear from you!

www.FindSomethingAwesome.com